the Three Sisters

Written by
Beth Larson Sherk

Illustrated by
Kevin Larson

RivannaRiver Books

please visit us at: rivannariverbooks.com

PRT0912A
Library of Congress Control Number: 2012942571
ISBN 10: 1620860910
ISBN 13: 9781620860915
Printed in the United States of America.

Once upon a time, not too long ago, there was a little girl named Amanda. She lived in a tall skinny house on the edge of town where the yellow fields rolled up into a tangle of forest.

One cold and lonely day, when spring was weak and not much comfort, she was sitting with her face pressed against the window, watching raindrops wriggle down the glass. Suddenly, something far off in the distance started moving up the Black Cat Road. What was it? It was so very small; she couldn't be sure. At first, it seemed like nothing more than three small shadows on the horizon, but when she looked again, they'd grown larger, twirling like whirlwinds. When she looked a third time she saw…

...three tall ladies in long gray skirts and black caps. Delicate black booted feet turned out just so, backs proudly arched, and necks stretching like long willow branches. But what seemed most odd about them was the way they walked in a line, bobbing their heads as if in time to a song no one else could hear.

    Could they be sisters? wondered Amanda.

    Suddenly, they all came to a stop as if with one mind and each reached down to pick a wild flower.

The little girl watched as the three strangers continued up the winding road right past her house.

Could they be heading into town? Suddenly, she was wide awake. She grabbed her yellow raincoat and rushed out the door just in time to see the last one disappearing around the bend.

There wasn't a moment to lose! "Come on, Boo!" She scooped up her orange cat and jumped on her bike. "Let's see what they're up to!"

She pedaled as fast as she could down Main Street and was just in time to see the three sisters go inside the town hall. Hundreds of birds were circling overhead, darkening the sky. The sound of their wings was like a mighty wind. Inside, there was a big meeting with the mayor and a little round man standing up in front, pointing at big charts.

"This is where we plan to build Paradise Hills," said the little round man. "Three hundred beautiful homes with a clubhouse, swimming pool, and - you guessed it - a golf course!"

The mayor and the little round man were smiling, patting each other on the back.

The three sisters stood in the outer hall listening and Amanda spied on them from behind the water fountain. Twittering birds perched on the ladies' shoulders and small creatures peeped out from under their long gray skirts. *Who were these strange ladies?*

"Folks, this town will never be the same!" announced the mayor. "This is what I call progress!"

The room echoed with the word, "Progress! Progress! Progress!"

It put the townspeople in a happy mood. The town would never be the same and that meant it was going to be better than ever - all because of progress!

That's when the three strangers, their delicate black booted feet turned out just so, backs proudly arched, necks stretched like long willow branches, headed straight up the aisle and sat in the very first row.

There were so many birds flying around the room that the people hardly noticed the three sisters. "How in the world did all these birds get in?" they cried in amazement.

"Any questions?" shouted the mayor over the hubbub.

With one motion the three sisters stood up, their voices ringing out over the confusion.

"What about the wild geese?"

"What will they do?"

"Where will they build their nests?"

Suddenly, everyone in the room was looking at them.

"And who are you?" asked the mayor.

"Ozamund," said the first.

"Winnowa," said the second.

"And Greshelda,"
said the third
in a dry, reedy voice.

"Are you saying we should stop progress for some silly birds?" The mayor and the little round man couldn't help but laugh, and all of the people laughed, too. It was just too ridiculous!

"Don't worry," said the mayor to the little round man. "The birds will just have to go somewhere else to build their nests. Otherwise, it wouldn't be fair to you. After all, you bought this land to make money!"

"That's right! It wouldn't be fair to him!" agreed the people among themselves.

"And it wouldn't be fair to the great people of this town who might want to live there!" he shouted in a booming voice.

"That's right!" they whispered to each other, "It wouldn't be fair to us!"

"But this is marshland," rang out a dry reedy voice. It was the first sister, Ozamund. "The wild geese have hatched their babies here long before man ever knew this place."

"Think, dear friends!" sang out the second sister, Winnowa. "Where will the wild geese cast their shadows on the land and who will hear their song when they are no more?"

"Beware!" chimed in the third sister, Greshelda. "Man's memory is short, but the Earth is old. Places more beautiful than this have turned to desert! Take care of the birds. Take care of the small creatures and the earth will take care of you."

With that the three sisters paraded down the aisle, their delicate black booted feet turned out just so, backs proudly arched, necks stretching like long willow branches.

The huge cloud of birds swirling above them gave a great cry and began flapping their wings as the three strangers marched out of the hall and into the street - stepping in every puddle on their way out of town.

Amanda pushed her way through the crowd of excited people, trying to catch up with the strange ladies. She jumped on her bike and pedaled as hard as she could. She went as fast as the wind, but the three sisters were faster still, walking in a perfect line, their heads bobbing to a song nobody else could hear.

Soon, they were only shadows on the horizon, but Amanda wasn't going to give up now! On and on she went until there was no one ahead of her and no one behind. She was all alone on the Black Cat Road. She'd never gone this far by herself before, but something inside made her know that she had to go on.

Around a curve and just over a hill, the Black Cat Road came to an end in a green glade of young saplings. In front, stood a proud wooden sign announcing:

PARADISE HILLS
-COMING SOON-

Through an opening in the trees, Amanda could see a marshy pond glittering in the sunlight. Among the tall bushes waving gently in the breeze, she saw the three sisters disappearing from sight.

"Wait! Come back!" cried Amanda. She threw down her bike and ran along the narrow path to catch up.

But when she got there, all she found was one long gray feather lying on the ground. "You dropped something!"

Suddenly, with a great flapping and honking, three wild geese rose up over the trees and lifted into the blue sky, their delicate black feet tucked underneath, their necks outstretched like long willow branches.

Amanda raised her hand with tears in her eyes. "Goodbye," she called out. "Have a safe journey. I hope I see you again!"

And the three sisters flew off into the sky and were soon out of sight.

Amanda headed back to her bike. She saw many creatures
peeping out of their hiding places
and she realized that this marshland was their home.

When Amanda returned to town, the meeting was still going on.

As soon as they saw her, a group of people gathered around. "What happened?" they asked.

"Three sisters visited us today and left us a gift," she said and lifted the feather for all to see.

"But what is it for?" someone asked. "You can't stuff a pillow with it!"

"You can't even dust furniture with it!" said another. "All you can do is look at it!"

The townspeople looked at the feather in Amanda's hand and wondered.

"Could it be," said an old voice, "that it was meant to remind us that the wild geese fly this way and that they belong here, too?"

Everyone was silent. This seemed like a very good reason, for who doesn't love a wild goose?

The mayor put his arm around the little round man and said, "I think I know a better place to build your Paradise Hills."

The little round man said, "Great! I'm all ears. I just want to build houses. I don't want to harm the wildlife or babies of any kind!"

Passing overhead, a flock of wild geese honked and flapped as three long gray feathers came drifting down to earth as if to say...goodbye.

the end

Marshlands are not waste lands!

Marshlands are *beautiful* places with many *different* kinds of plants and animals, giving us and all the critters **fresh** water to drink and **oxygen** to breathe!

Did you know that marshlands, swamps, fens, and **bogs** are all wetlands?

A wetland, marshland, swamp, fen, or bog is a place where the **soil is saturated with water** all year round or only at certain times during the year. These wetland areas may be completely covered with shallow pools of water, or they may have only certain parts covered with water.

Marshlands are Nature's Sponge!

Marshlands filter the water to make it clean, soak up extra water after heavy rains, and keep streams from flooding!

One acre of wetlands can store 1 to 1.5 million gallons of water!

A wetland one mile wide can reduce a **storm surge** by 1 to 1.5 feet.

A **storm surge** is water being pushed by a storm, like a hurricane, and becoming so deep that it becomes like a flood, which can be bad for people and animals.

The water found in wetlands can be saltwater as in the ocean, freshwater as in lakes, rivers and streams, or brackish water. Brackish water is more salt then fresh, but still not as salty as seawater.

Did you know there are more kinds of plants and animals in a wetland than any other kind of ecosystem?

These plants love to grow in wetlands:
Mangrove, water lilies, cattails, sedges, tamarack, black spruce, cypress, gum, pondweed, duckweed, watermeal, bladderwort, arrowhead, and many others.

The **world's largest wetland** is the *Pantanal* in *South America*. It is actually a large floodplain that covers between 54,000 to 75,000 square miles! A floodplain is *flat land* beside a river or stream and, like the bottom of a swimming pool, is able to hold vast amounts of water. During the rainy season, 80% of the *Pantanal floodplain* is under water and nurtures an incredibly diverse collection of aquatic plants and animals.

Marshlands are a home and visiting place for many kinds of water birds.

But did you know that all these animals live in marshlands too?

Amphibians (frogs, toads, newts, salamanders, and others.)

Reptiles (turtles, tortoises, snakes, lizards, crocodiles, alligators, and more.)

Mammals (beavers, deer, moose, foxes, panthers, and others.)

Birds (geese, ducks, swans, herons, owls, eagles, falcons, and many others.)

Crustaceans (crabs, lobsters, shrimp, and more.)

Also insects (spiders, mosquitoes, crickets, etc.)

Remember, all wetlands are important!

The **conservation movement** *aims* to **protect** the places where plants and animals live. (Find out more on the last page of this book.)

Definitions:
Wildlife = animals and plants that naturally grow in a region
Organism = a plant or animal or single-celled life form
Ecosystems = a community of interacting organisms
Biology = the study of living organisms
Fauna = the animals of a particular region (area)
Saturated = soaked with liquid
Nurture = helping something to grow

Coloring pages! ▶

Websites to visit:

Ducks Unlimited
World leader in Wetlands Conservation
www.ducks.org

Wildlife Conservation Society
www.wcs.org

National Wildlife Federation
www.nwf.org

World Wildlife fund
www.wwf.org

visit **Wiki Wetland** on the internet and find more great information on wetlands.